Jon Scieszka's TRUCKTOWN

TAKE A TRIP WITH TRUCKTOWN!

James

WRITTEN BY **JUSTIN SPELVIN**

CHARACTERS AND ENVIRONMENTS DEVELOPED BY THE

DAVID SHANNON   **LOREN LONG**   **DAVID GORDON**

SIMON & SCHUSTER BOOKS FOR YOUNG READERS
NEW YORK   LONDON   TORONTO   SYDNEY

SIMON & SCHUSTER BOOKS FOR YOUNG READERS
An imprint of Simon & Schuster Children's Publishing Division
1230 Avenue of the Americas, New York, New York 10020
Copyright © 2011 by JRS Worldwide, LLC.
TRUCKTOWN and JON SCIESZKA'S TRUCKTOWN
and design are trademarks of JRS Worldwide, LLC.
All rights reserved, including the right of reproduction in whole or in part in any form.
SIMON & SCHUSTER BOOKS FOR YOUNG READERS is a trademark of Simon & Schuster, Inc.
For information about special discounts for bulk purchases, please contact Simon & Schuster Special
Sales at 1-866-506-1949 or business@simonandschuster.com.
The Simon & Schuster Speakers Bureau can bring authors to your live event.
For more information or to book an event, contact the Simon & Schuster Speakers Bureau
at 1-866-248-3049 or visit our website at www.simonspeakers.com.
Book design by Tom Daly
The text for this book is set in Truck King.
The illustrations for this book are digitally rendered.
Manufactured in the United States of America
0111 LAK
2 4 6 8 10 9 7 5 3 1
ISBN 978-1-4169-4181-1

Created by Jon Scieszka. Characters and environments developed by the

David Shannon, Loren Long, and David Gordon.
Illustration crew: Executive Producer: TOT Industries in association with Animagic S.L.
Creative Supervisor: Sergio Pablos.
Drawings by: Juan Pablo Navas. Color by: Isabel Nadal. Color Assistant: Gabriela Lazbal.
Art Director: Tom Daly.

One morning while the gang was hanging out at the garbage dump,
Gabriella had an important announcement.
"I'm bored," she said. "Bored. Bored. Bored."
"Why don't we smash something!" said Jack.
"Nah," said Gabby. "I want to do something new."
No one could think what to do.

"How about you go on a road trip!" suggested Rosie.
"What a great idea," said Gabby. "We could go to the country."
"All new sights," said Rosie. "All new sounds."
"All new smells!" said Gabby.
"I'd come with you, but I have a ton of stuff to wreck today," said Rosie.
"I'd come with you," said Melvin, "but trips make me worried."

Everyone else agreed a road trip to the country
was just the way to spend the day.
"V–V–Varooooommm!" said Max. "I am excited to the max!"

"A trip to the country!" honked Dan. "Fresh air! New roads!
I can't wait to find brand-new dirt to dump."

"Getting there is half the fun," said Jack.
"Let's race. Let's roll. Last one there is a rotten tire."

Gabby was very excited. Big Rig—well, Big Rig wasn't.
"Come with us, Big Rig," said Gabby. "We're going on a road trip.
We're headed to the country. We'll see all kinds of things and play all
kinds of games. We're going to race down cool new roads. We're going
to smell all new smells. We're going to . . ."
"No," said Big Rig.
And that was that.

The gang was off on a road trip. Racing and riding, heading to the country. Gabby wanted to get there first! "I wonder what we're going to find there," she said as she zoomed.

They found out that things were very different from busy, booming, bustling Trucktown. There were no buildings, no bridges, no highways, and no tunnels. The only sounds they heard were their own engines roaring. Gabby smelled something strange. "What is that smell?" she asked. "Fresh grass," said Max.

"Which is *so* much fun to play in. Let's go off-roading!" shouted Jack. Jack peeled out, and took off. "You gotta love the country," he cheered.

Around the corner they found more trees
than Gabby had ever seen before.
"Where are we?" she asked.

"It's an apple orchard," said Dan.
"Wow, something smells funny," said Gabby.
"That's all the fresh apples," said Dan. "I'm going to catch as many as I can.
Watch: one, two, three . . ."
Gabby rolled on. She knew Dan would be counting *all day*.

A little ways away was the perfect racing hill. They each took
a turn to see who could make it down the fastest.
Izzy revved his engines. He spun his wheels. He flew down the hill until—
BAM!—he bumped into a rock. And—BOOM!—he bounced into the air.
"Are you all right, Izzy?" asked Jack.
"Do you want an ice cream? Do you want an ice cream?
Do you want an ice cream?" Izzy replied.
"Whew!" said Gabby. "He's all right."

But then Gabby smelled the weirdest, strangest, craziest
smell she'd ever smelled. "Whoa!" she said.
"Gabby, you've smelled flowers before," said Dan.
"Not this many!" said Gabby. "Not all at once."

The air smelled so sweet, Gabby couldn't even remember what garbage smelled like. Maybe it was time to head home. There was just one small problem.
"Uh-oh, looks like Gabby is sinking," said Jack.

Once Gabby was unstuck, it was definitely time to head back.
"I had a great time in the country," she said, "but I am starting to miss Trucktown."

On the drive back the gang talked about all the things they missed.
They missed the roads and the ramps, the sights and the sounds.
"But," said Gabby, "there's one thing I miss most of all. . . ."

"The smell of home!"